The FISH from
JAPAN

THE FiSH FROM JAPAN

Elizabeth K. Cooper

With pictures by Beth and Joe Krush

HARCOURT, BRACE & WORLD, INC., NEW YORK

also by Elizabeth K. Cooper

SCIENCE IN YOUR OWN BACK YARD

DISCOVERING CHEMISTRY

SCIENCE ON THE SHORES AND BANKS

SILKWORMS AND SCIENCE: *The Story of Silk*

INSECTS AND PLANTS: *The Amazing Partnership*

AND EVERYTHING NICE: *The Story of Sugar, Spice, and Flavoring*

MINERALS (with Herbert S. Zim)

WHO IS PADDY? (with Harriet Pincus)

*To children who have pets,
and to children who wish they had pets*

Harvey was early. He slipped into the room and looked around. No one, not even the teacher, was there. He ran to the glass tank and picked up the turtle.

"Hi, turtle!" said Harvey.

The little green turtle sat in Harvey's hand and blinked its eyes.

Karl rushed in and saw Harvey with the turtle.
"Put that down!" he shouted. "That's my turtle!"
Harvey put the turtle back into the tank.
"I think it likes me," he said.

Karl began to feed his turtle.

"I wish I could help," said Harvey.

But Karl said, "No! Nobody else can feed my turtle. Go feed your own pets."

He went on feeding the turtle, and all Harvey could do was watch.

"I don't have a pet," Harvey said in a minute.

"Then get one," Karl replied.

"I wish I could," answered Harvey. "I'll ask my mother again, but I don't think it will do any good."

Harvey was right. When he asked his mother, she said the same old things. She had no time and no money for pets. She had all she could do just taking care of Harvey.

"But look," she said. "Here's a letter from Uncle Albert. He has a surprise for you."

There were six strange-looking stamps on the envelope. "It came all the way across the ocean," said Harvey's mother. "Uncle Albert is going to send you a fish from Japan."

"A fish! When will I get it?" asked Harvey.

"Any day, any day," said his mother.

Harvey could hardly wait to tell his friends.

The next morning in school, Harvey did something he had never done before. He went to the front of the room and stood before the teacher and all the children. And he spoke so everyone could hear him.

"I am getting a pet!" he announced. "My uncle is

sending me a fish from Japan. When it comes, I will bring it to school to show."

The children were almost as eager as Harvey to see a fish from Japan, and so was the teacher.

At supper that night, Harvey's mother dished out some ice cream. "I need that jar when it's empty," said Harvey.

"Here's one that's already empty," said his mother.

"That's not the right kind," said Harvey. "I want a jar I can see through, like glass."

"Oh, you mean transparent," said his mother. "I'll wash this one out, and then you can have it."

Harvey took the transparent jar to the bathroom, filled it with water, and carried it to his room. Then he sat in front of the jar and looked into the water. He was ready for his fish from Japan.

But the fish did not come, not the next day nor the next nor the next.

Each morning in school the children would ask, "Did you get your pet, Harvey? Did you get the fish from Japan?"

All Harvey could say was, "No, not yet. But the water is ready, and so is the jar. I think the fish will be here tomorrow."

Some children laughed at Harvey. "He'll never get that fish!" said Karl. "He just made it up."

But one day the fish really came. It came in a big envelope with many stamps.

"It must be a very flat fish," said Harvey to himself.
"I hope it's not too big for my jar."

He ran to his room, opening the envelope.

There, at last, was the fish from Japan! It was made of colored paper and had a long string fastened to its mouth. It was a kite, the kind that Japanese children like to fly.

Harvey looked at the kite. Then he folded it up, put it back into the envelope, and hid it under some things in his closet.

Harvey sat down and looked and looked at the water in the transparent jar. If only the fish had been tiny and alive! Harvey could almost see it swimming around and around in the jar. Now what was he going to tell the other children in school?

The next morning Harvey put a lid on the jar and took it to school early. He crept into the room and put the jar next to the turtle tank. As he was taking off the lid, Karl came in.

"What's that?" asked Karl.

"That's my fish from Japan," said Harvey. "It came yesterday."

Just then the bell rang, and the teacher came in with the children.

"Harvey said that's his fish!" cried Karl. "But I can't see any fish."

"Of course not," said Harvey. "It's transparent."

"What kind of fish?" asked the teacher.

"Transparent," said Harvey. "That means you can see right through it. It's hard to see a transparent fish in water."

Harvey took a small box from his pocket. "My fish

eats transparent food," he said to the teacher. "I have to feed it three times a day, like this."

The teacher and all the children watched as Harvey fed his fish.

"Will you let me feed it sometime?" asked Karl.

"Maybe," said Harvey, "when you learn how."

At free time the children crowded around Harvey's jar. They all tried to see the transparent fish.

"There's nothing there but plain water," said a girl.

"But look, the water's moving!" said another girl. "That's where the fish is swimming and turning. It makes a tiny, tiny ripple."

"I almost saw it, too!" cried Karl.

Karl stared and stared at the water. Suddenly he shouted, "I think I saw one eye! It was round and shiny, and it looked right at me! You have to look hard to see it."

The children looked very hard. Then a boy cried out, "I saw the other eye! I really did!"

All the children looked harder than ever. They were very quiet until one boy began to jump up and down.

"I just saw the fins!" he said. "They're like little fans, and they go back and forth, like this." The boy used his hands to show how the fins moved in the water.

"Did you see the tail?" asked a girl. "There, in that sunny spot! It's long and wavy and has lots of colors. There! I just saw it again."

"So did I! So did I!" said the other children.

The children stared at the jar, and the teacher stared at the children.

"I never heard of this kind of fish before," she said.
Harvey looked up and smiled. "It's a very rare fish,"
he said. "It came all the way from Japan."

"Look at the mouth!" shouted a boy. "It opens and shuts, opens and shuts."

And the boy made a funny fish mouth with his lips. Another boy made a fish mouth with his hands.

"I think the fish is hungry," said Harvey. "Stand back. I'm going to feed it."

As he opened his little box of transparent food, he looked over at Karl. "You can feed it this time," said Harvey.

"Thanks, Harve!" said Karl, and he fed the fish from Japan.

Harvey said that the fish needed rest after its lunch. The children tiptoed back to their seats, and the teacher put out the painting things.

The children began to paint. Everyone made a picture of Harvey's fish.

When the paintings were dry, the teacher put them
up on the wall.

"Do you like them, Harvey?" she asked.

"What a fish!" said Harvey. "What a wonderful fish!"

When school was over, Harvey took his fish jar home
with him.

The next morning Harvey came to school without the jar. The children ran to meet him.

"Where is your fish?" they asked.

"Gone!" said Harvey. "A cat sneaked into my room last night, and it ate the fish from Japan."

"That was awful," said Karl. And then he asked, "Want to help feed my turtle?"

"Sure!" said Harvey. "We can feed it together."

And that is what they did.